HAPPY HATS

Peter Curry

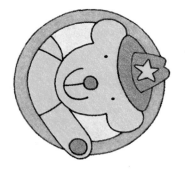

Scholastic Publications Ltd.
10 Earlham Street, London WC2H 9RX, UK

Scholastic Inc.,
730 Broadway, New York, NY 10003, USA

Scholastic Canada Ltd.,
123 Newkirk Road, Richmond Hill,
Ontario L4C 3G5, Canada

Ashton Scholastic Pty. Ltd.
P O Box 579, Gosford, New South Wales,
Australia

Ashton Scholastic Ltd.,
Private Bag 1, Penrose, Auckland
New Zealand

First published by Scholastic Publications Ltd., 1990
First published in paperback 1991

Text copyright © Peter Curry, 1990

ISBN 0 590 76423 3

All rights reserved

Made and printed in Belgium
by Proost International Book Production

HAPPY HATS

Peter Curry

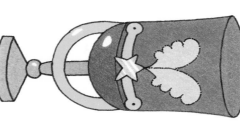

Hippo Books
Scholastic Publications Limited
London

If your head would like
a hat on the top,
come and choose one
from the *Happy Hats* shop.

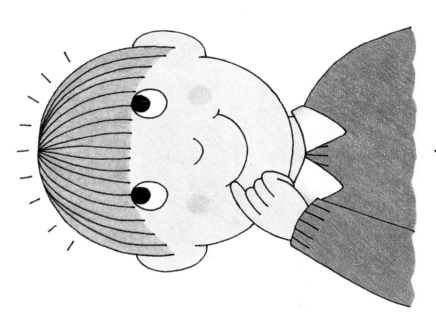

A hat with fruit
may well suit you,
but do take care
down at the zoo!

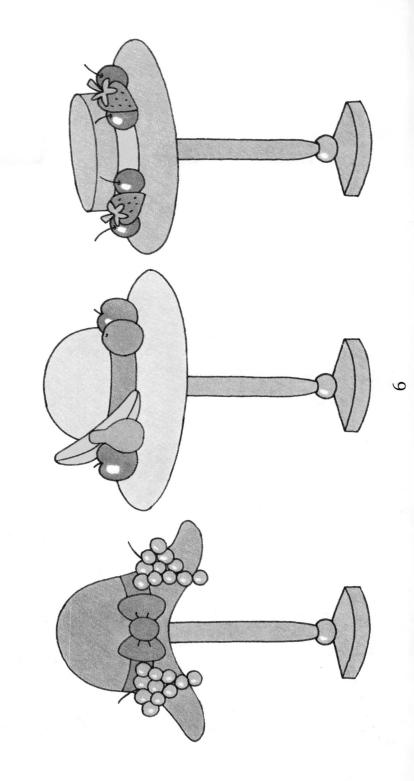

Striped sun-hats
are specially made
to keep your head
in nice cool shade.

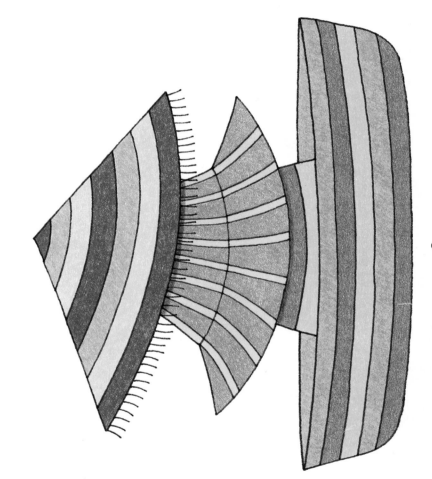

Choose a hat
to sail your boat.
Be a jolly sailor
or a pirate afloat.

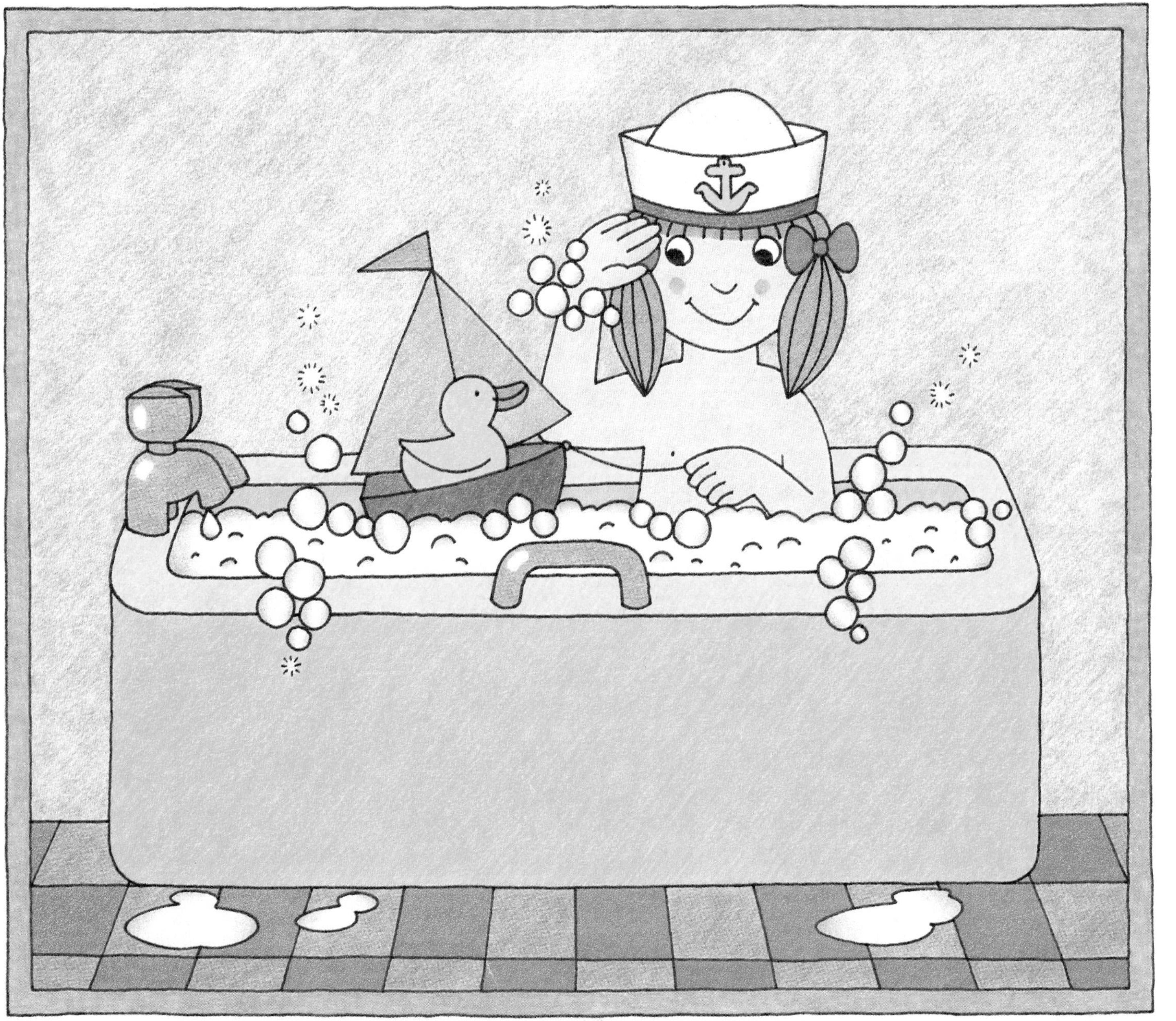

Magic hats –
take your pick,
and *hey presto!*
an amazing trick!

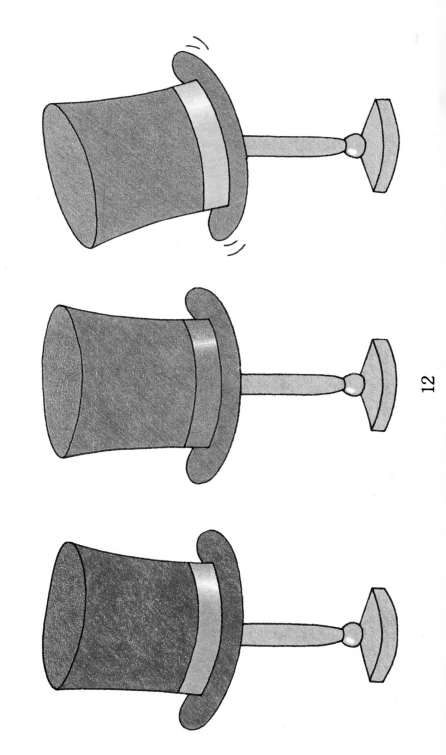

Party hats
for party fun.
A jolly hat
for everyone.

PARTY TIME

Warm knitted hats
for frost and snow
will turn sh-sh-shivers
into a glow.

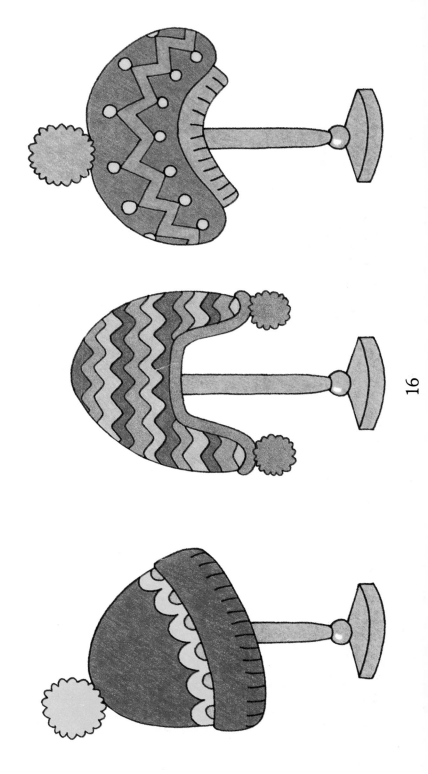

With a witch's hat
you should take care,
or come Hallowe'en
there might be a scare!

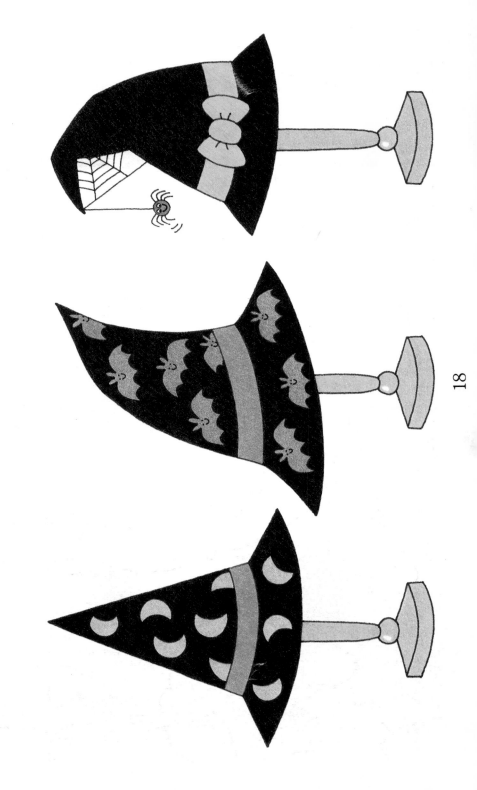

Be a clown
with a funny hat
and everyone
will laugh at that!

Pretty straw bonnets
trimmed with a posy
will make butterflies
and busy bees nosy.

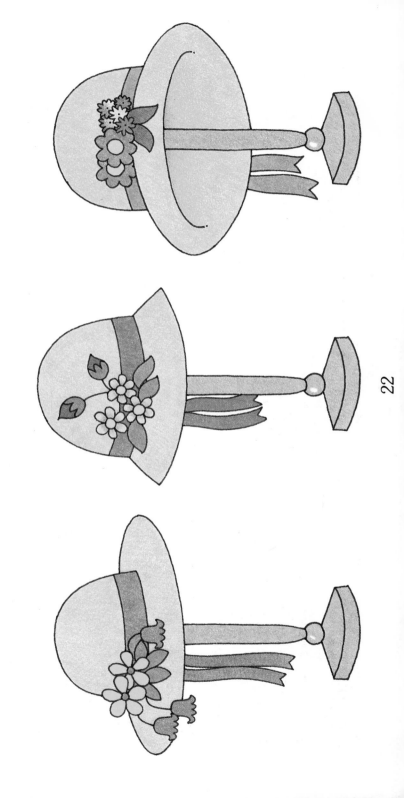

There are fine sou'westers
on sale this week,
should you need a hat
which will not leak.

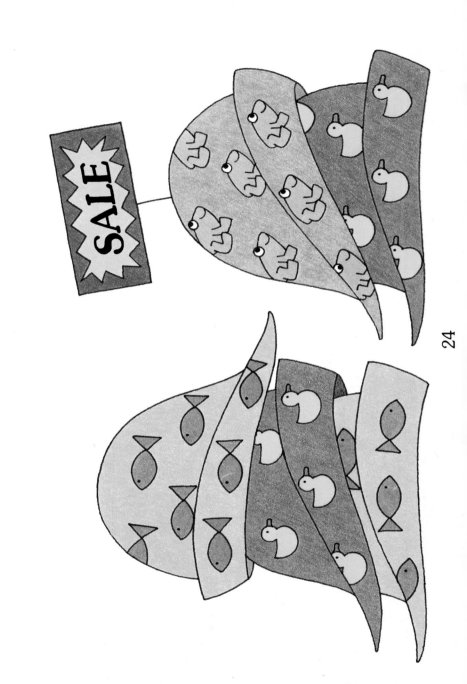

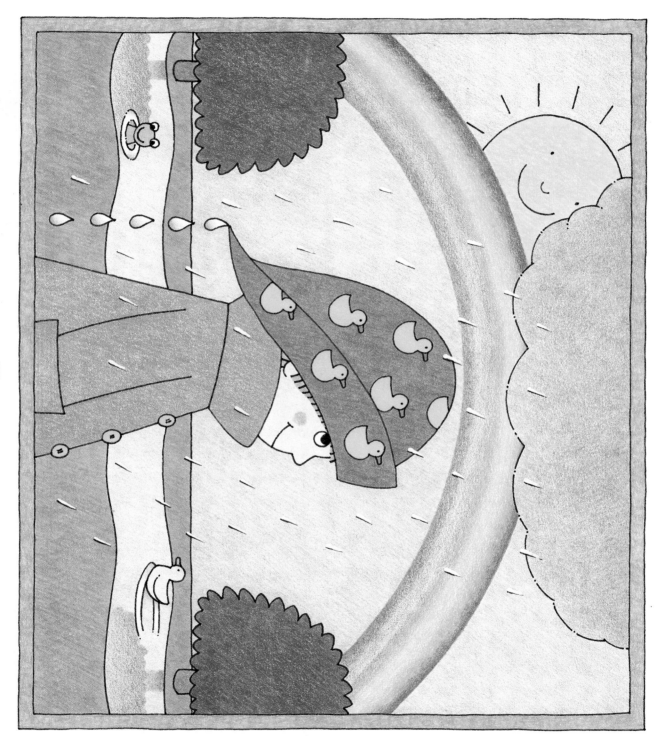

Soft nightcaps
for sleepyheads,
to keep them cosy
in their beds.

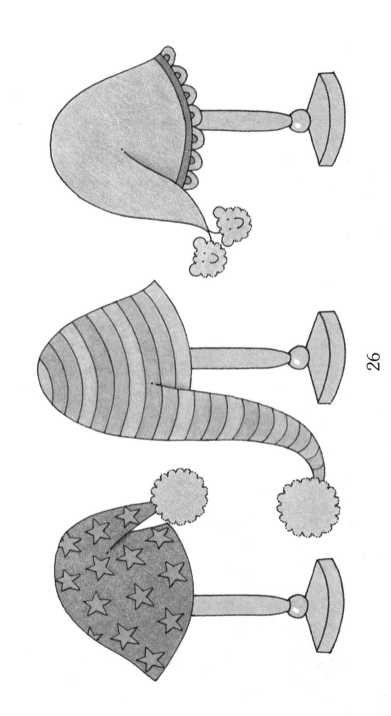

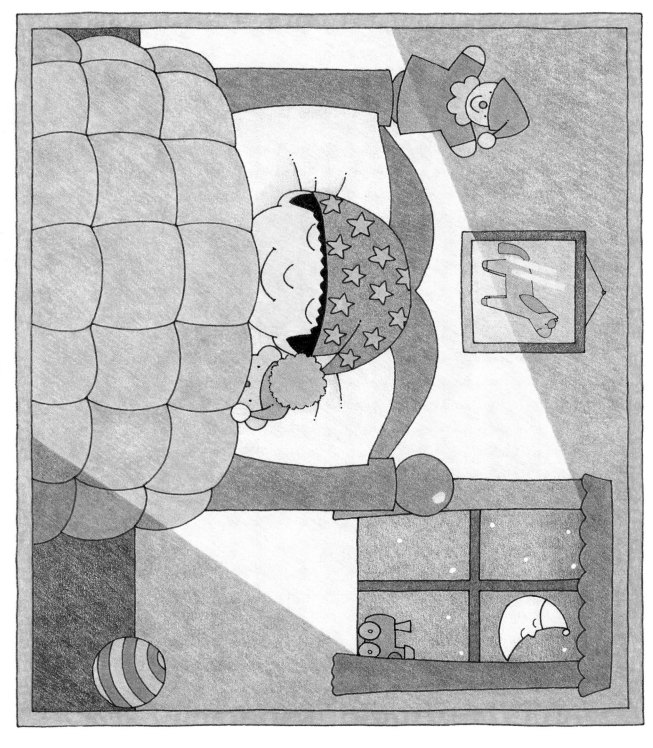

With silver stars
and golden braid,
these hats are dressed
for a big parade.

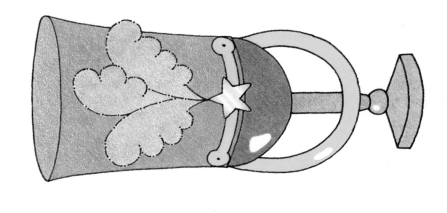

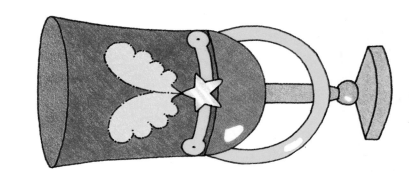

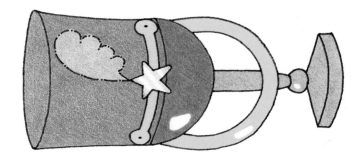

Now if your head
still has no hat,
the lucky dip
will soon fix that!

LUCKY
DIP

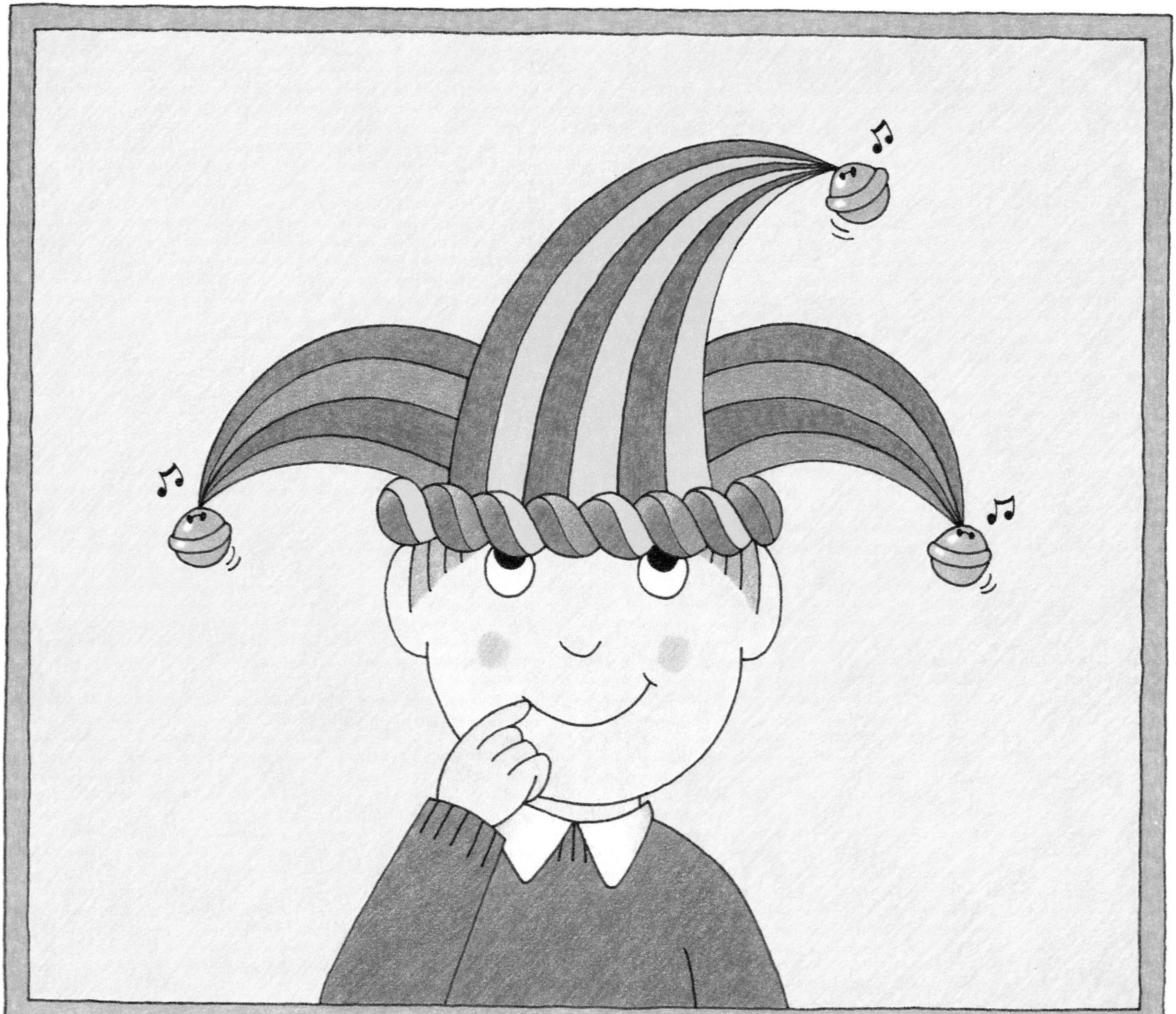